Wheels

Hollywood

Junkyard

Clips

Google-Eyes

Einstein

The Dunderheads

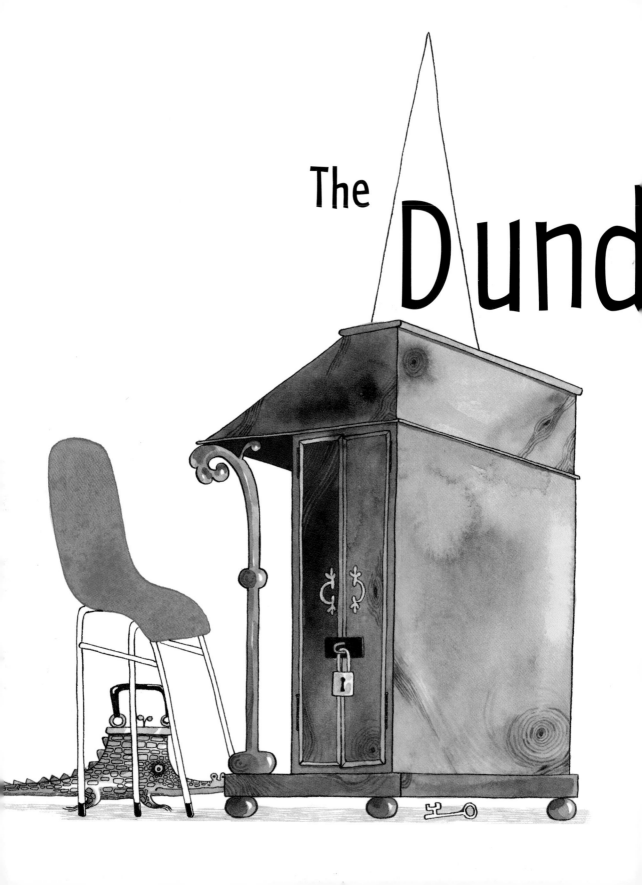

The Dund

erheads

PAUL FLEISCHMAN

illustrated by DAVID ROBERTS

CANDLEWICK PRESS

First edition 2009

Library of Congress Cataloging-in-Publication Data is available.

Library of Congress Catalog Card Number 2008934579

ISBN 978-0-7636-2498-9

2 4 6 8 10 9 7 5 3

Printed in China

This book was typeset in Esprit.
The illustrations were done in watercolor, pen, and ink.

Candlewick Press
99 Dover Street
Somerville, Massachusetts 02144

visit us at www.candlewick.com

For Milton Love
P. F.

For Auntie Barbara
D. R.

"Never," shrieked Miss Breakbone, "have I been asked to teach such a scraping-together of fiddling, twiddling, time-squandering, mind-wandering, doodling, dozing, don't-knowing dunderheads!"

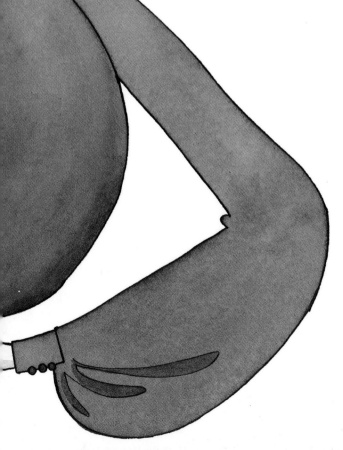

That was her first mistake: the insult.

Mistake Number 2: no eye for talent. An easy mistake to make, in our case.

Miss Breakbone hated kids. Every time she made a student cry, she gave herself a gold star.

Confiscating was her specialty.

Rumor had it she'd bought her electric chair from selling all the stuff she'd taken away.

Then, one Friday, she went too far.

"Theodore! Bring that magnifying glass up here this instant!"

She didn't know that everyone called him Junkyard. He was always digging stuff out of trash cans—

like the one-eared cat he'd found when we'd walked to school that morning. You should have seen his face light up.

His mother was a maniac
for cat stuff, and he'd
needed a present for her
birthday that Sunday.
He was set.

"*And* the cat!" snapped Miss Breakbone.
Mistake Number 3:
the outrage.

Junkyard put them both on her desk. And then he started crying, right in front of the girls. Miss Breakbone gave herself a gold star.

"But they're mine," he said.

"Not anymore," she snapped. She studied the cat's green eyes with interest. "And don't even *think* about getting them back!"

Mistake Number 4: the dare.

She locked them in a drawer and smiled. Junkyard looked my way, begging me. I knew what he wanted. Everyone called me Einstein because I was a whiz at solving problems. But something told me that this would be tougher than anything I'd ever tackled. I thought it over. Then I nodded. I'd show her what a few dunderheads could do.

At recess, they were all around me.

"It's impossible! She keeps the keys on her belt!"

"Then she takes the stuff home!"

"We don't even know where she lives!"

"She reads *Guard Dog Lovers Monthly*!"

I was going to need help.

Lots of it.

At lunch, I talked to Wheels.

He's kind of a bicycle nut. He'd put forty-eight extra gears on his bike that summer,

not to mention a reclining seat, turn signals, speakers, and a water fountain.

He didn't have any problem after school keeping up with Breakbone's car.

Breakbone's house

School

"The place is like a castle! You'll never get in!"

He gave me her address.

"That's what she thinks," I said. I needed more info.
Then I remembered Pencil.

She sees something once,

she can draw it from memory.

I sent her out to Breakbone's house.
She did the outside first.

For the inside, she threw a paper airplane over the wall. Breakbone's maid led her through most of the ground floor to get to the backyard.

The drawings hit my desk before dinner.

By bedtime, I had it worked out.

On Saturday morning, I left the house early. It was time to put the team together.

My first stop was Spider's. The best way to find him is to look up. I guess it's something he got from his family.

"Can you help me out on a little project tonight?"

"What kind of project?"

"The kind that could be hazardous to your health."

"Excellent," he said. "What time?"

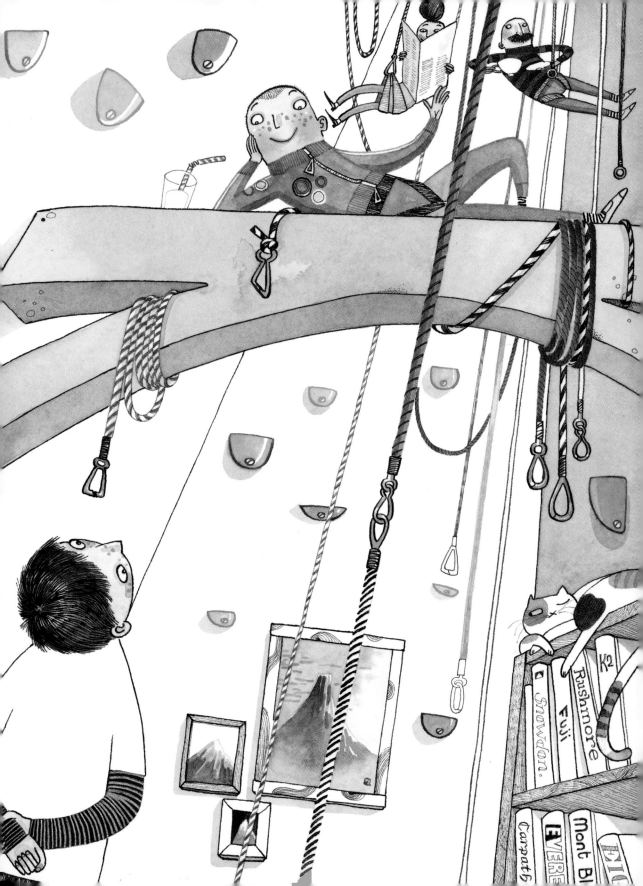

EAST SIDE ANECDOTE

AN AUSTRALIAN WEREWOLF IN LUTON

I walked around the block to Hollywood's. She's got every movie that was ever made and has watched them all eleven times. I had a feeling she'd come in handy.

"You busy tonight?"

"It's Saturday, of course I'm busy, I'm going to the movies, what do you think, then I'm coming home, and first I'm gonna watch—"

It took some doing, but I talked her into it.

Spitball was a little tougher.
He could spit farther than anyone in
the school—until a new kid had moved
to town last spring and beaten him by an inch
and three-eighths. He was still shaken up.

"I don't know," he moaned.
"What good would I be?"
"Plenty," I said. "I've got
a slot just for you."
I signed him up.
Likewise the rest
of the crew.

Spitball's record

Wheels picked us up at eight sharp.

When we got there,
we were in luck.
Bad luck. Breakbone
was having a party.

"We'll get caught for sure!"

"Let's try tomorrow!"

"Junkyard needs that cat tomorrow," I said.
"We're going in tonight." I turned to Spider.
"See if anyone's in the backyard."

There was an elm tree on one side of the
house. Spider shot up it like an elevator.

"All clear," he called down.

I nodded to Clips. His reading scores were low.
His math scores were worse. But if they tested
for paper-clip chains . . .

"Just like you asked for." He opened his briefcase. "Two eight-strand ten-footers, fisherman's weave, with grappling hooks."

We were on the other side in a flash. It was pitch-black. No one could see — except Hollywood. She'd spent so much time in theaters that she had perfect night vision. I put her at the front.

Suddenly she stopped. "Something's going to happen," she said. "I can just tell. Something scary."

"This isn't a movie," I said. "It's —"

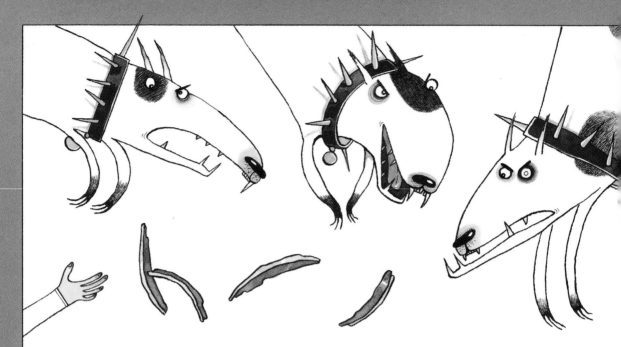

That's when the four guard dogs charged toward us.
Pencil had told me all about them. I looked back at
Junkyard. "Now!"

He whipped out the pork ribs he'd
found in the trash and threw
one to each dog. They stopped
where they were and
started gnawing.

That's when Google-Eyes went to work. The year before, she'd found a book on hypnotism in the school library. On her way out, she'd put the librarian in a two-week trance. Over the summer, she'd done a lot of experimenting on her younger brother. The dogs dropped like marionettes.

We slipped into the garage.

"Over here!" said Clips.

And there they were, in a box marked SELL —
the phones and pocketknives and radios and
everything else Breakbone had taken that year.
Everything, that is, except the one-eared cat.

"Maybe it's worth something," said Junkyard.

I'd already had the same thought. "My guess is
she put it in a safe. We'll need to go in. If only
we knew what room the—"

"Master bedroom," said Hollywood. *"Obviously."*

She was annoying, but she gave good advice.

I studied Pencil's plans. "Second floor."

We crept out. Suddenly, the motion lights hit us.
I saw Breakbone in the kitchen.

"Spitball — now! Give it everything you've got!"

He popped a piece of bread in his mouth,
gave it a chew, took in a huge breath, then spit it
toward the house.

It shot through th

ight air,

then stuck square on the sensor — keeping it from picking up our movements. It was the greatest feat of spitting ever seen.

"Nice work," I said. The lights went out.

"The house is full of people," said Junkyard. "How do we get in?"

I nodded to Clips. He joined his two chains into one. Spider went up the drainpipe like malt up a straw, then hooked the chain to a second-floor balcony. A minute later, we were inside the castle's walls, in a bedroom with sheets on the furniture.

"Must be a guest room," said Clips. "Where's the master bedroom?"

The plans only covered the ground floor. But I'd studied the pattern of windows and had a rough idea of the layout.

"This way," I said. I opened a door. And there was the party, right below us.

We had to crawl to keep from being seen. Hollywood tugged my pant leg. "I'm getting this bad feeling, like something's—"

I looked around. A maid was coming up the stairs straight toward us. Spitball saw her, too. He gathered his saliva and took aim at an empty glass down below. Direct hit. It fell to the floor and shattered.

"Josephine!" shouted Breakbone. "Clean this up first!"

The maid turned around. It wouldn't take long to clean up the glass. We'd have to be fast.

We crawled down the hall and into a room.
The master bedroom.

"The safe's always behind a painting," said
Hollywood.

I lifted the only painting off the wall. No safe.

"This movie's weird," she said.

"The maid will be back any second," I said. "Everybody look!"

Clips only thinks about paper clips.

He saw one on the floor, bent down to get it, bumped his head on the wall—

and suddenly that section of wall turned around. And there before us was a bolted-down strongbox.

"Cool," he said.

The box was locked. It was Nails's turn to shine.

He spends a lot of time on his fingernails, filing them into different shapes—

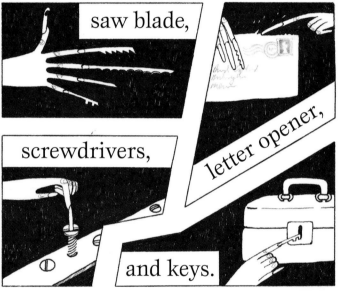

saw blade, screwdrivers, letter opener, and keys.

Unfortunately, none of them fit the lock. Fortunately, he keeps one long and untouched, just for such special occasions. With his clipper and file, he turned it into a custom key.

The box opened. And there was the cat. "Back to your owner," I said. I tossed it to Junkyard and dropped a little something in its place. "Now let's scram."

Then the bedroom door opened. And there stood the maid.

She was so frightened, no words came out when she screamed. Instantly, Spider pulled her in and shut the door. Google-Eyes jumped up on the bed, put her face in front of the maid's, and gave her the Express Trance. Five seconds later, the maid fell straight back.

"Let's go," I said. We went out the way we came in. Wheels was outside waiting. Junkyard's smile told him the mission had been a success.

On Sunday, Junkyard's mom got the one-eared cat.

Those strange green eyes turned out to be emeralds. Worth a lot of money.

She gave Junkyard a big gift certificate to an ice cream shop by way of thanks. He invited me along.

"There's just one thing I've been wondering," he said. "What was that you put in Breakbone's box?"

"Just a little letter to our teacher," I replied.

Hollywood

Wheels

Junkyard

Clips

Google-Eyes

Einstein